PLANES

by Anne Rockwell

E. P. Dutton • New York

Published in the United States by E. P. Dutton, Inc.,
2 Park Avenue, New York, N.Y. 10016

Published simultaneously in Canada by
Fitzhenry & Whiteside Limited, Toronto

Editor: Ann Durell   Designer: Isabel Warren-Lynch

Printed in Hong Kong by South China Printing Co.
First Edition COBE 10 9 8 7 6 5 4 3 2 1

Library of Congress Cataloging in Publication Data

Rockwell, Anne F.
  Planes.

  Summary: Simple text and illustrations introduce
different types of airplanes.
  1. Airplanes—Pictorial works—Juvenile literature.
[1. Airplanes] I. Title.
TL547.R57 1985 629.133′34 84-13732
ISBN 0-525-44159-X

Planes fly in the sky.

They fly over mountains
and over farms.

They fly over cities
and oceans too.

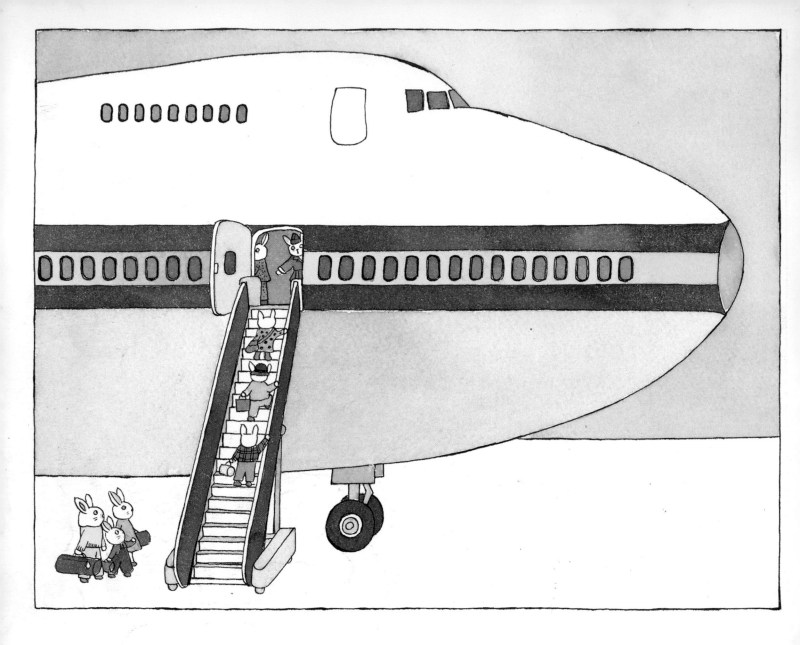

There are big planes

and little planes.

Seaplanes with pontoons can land on water.

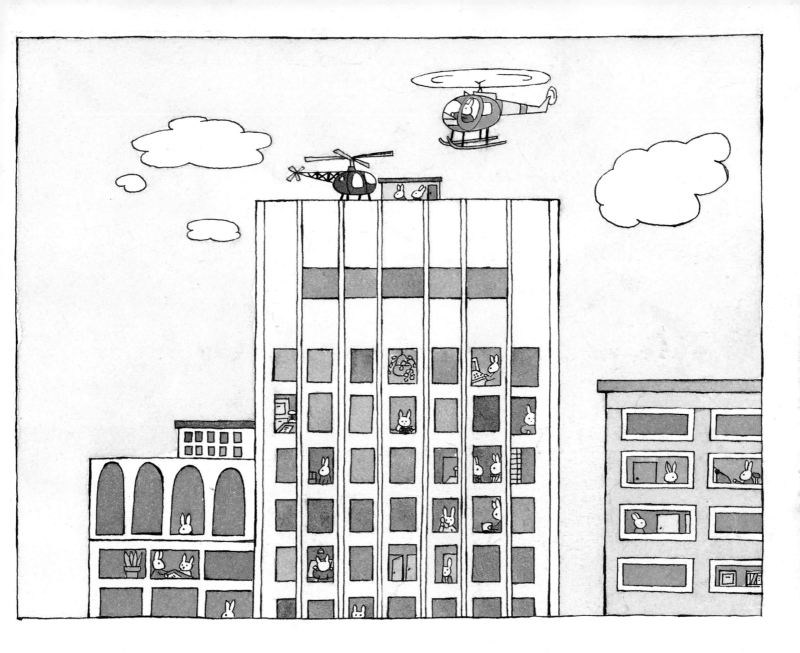

Helicopters can land on skyscraper rooftops.

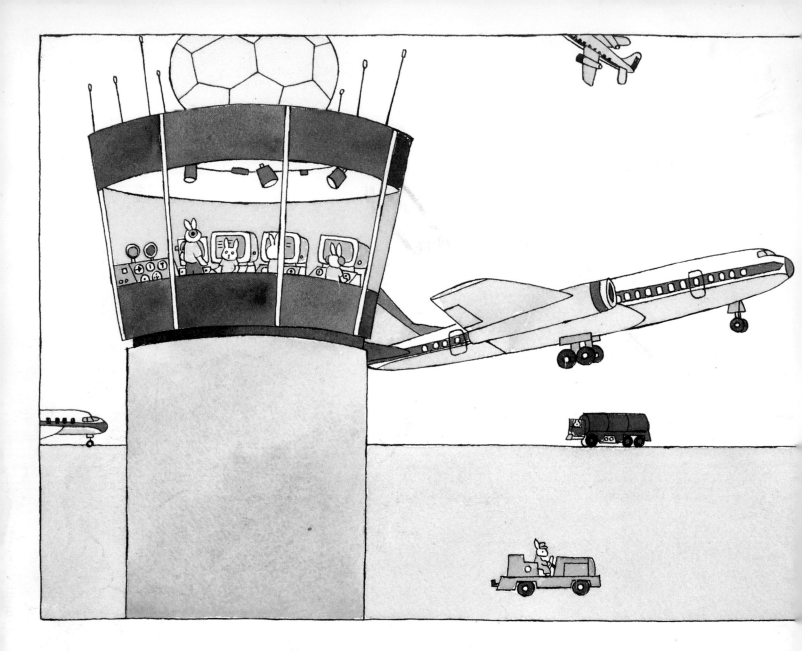

But most planes take off

and land at busy airports.

There are old planes

and new planes.

There are model airplanes,

and some of them can fly.

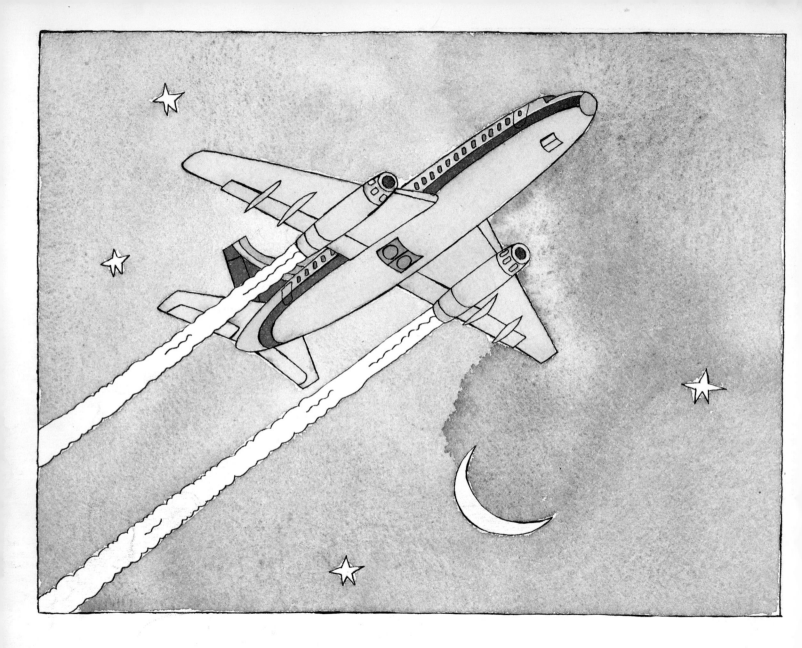

Jet engines make some planes go.

Whirling propellers make others go.

Wind makes a hang glider go.

Pilots fly planes.

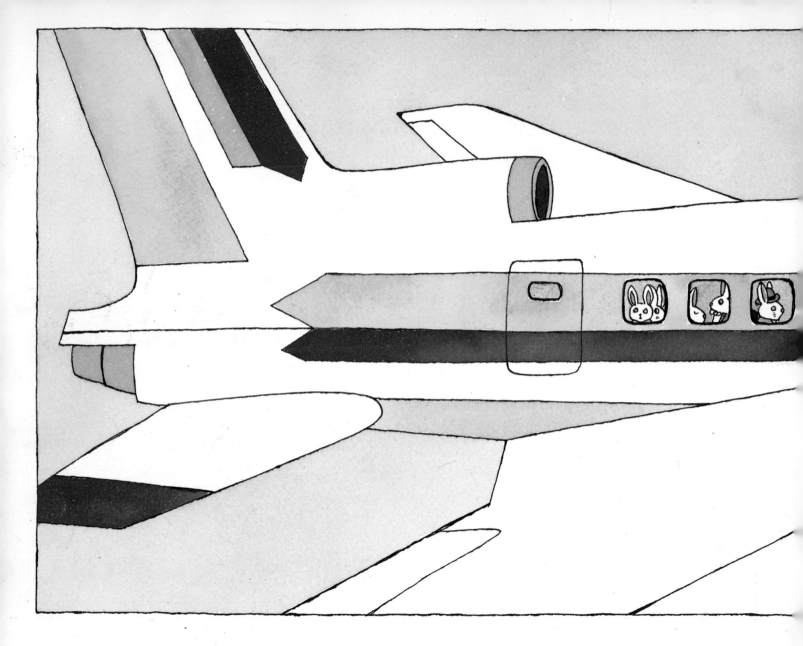

We ride in planes.

From the North Pole

to the South Pole—all around the world—

planes fly in the sky.